Honey & Mahogany

written by
Heather R. Phillips

Mill City Press, Inc.
2301 Lucien Way #415
Maitland, FL 32751
407.339.4217
www.millcitypress.net

© 2021 by Heather R. Phillips

All rights reserved. No part of this publication may be reproduced, stored in a retrieval system, or transmitted, in any form or by any means, electronic, mechanical, photocopying, recording, or otherwise, without the prior written permission of the author.

Due to the changing nature of the Internet, if there are any web addresses, links, or URLs included in this manuscript, these may have been altered and may no longer be accessible. The views and opinions shared in this book belong solely to the author and do not necessarily reflect those of the publisher. The publisher, therefore, disclaims responsibility for the views or opinions expressed within the work.

Library of Congress Control Number:

Paperback ISBN-13: 978-1-66282-871-3
Ebook ISBN-13: 978-1-66282-872-0

I dedicate this book to all of the honey bronze, rich mahogany, and all beautiful shades in between of children who are all God's lovely and perfect children.

Thank you to my family for supporting my dreams and embracing my desire to radiate this dark world with light and love.

Thank you to God who has created a beautiful and colorful world.

~Heather R. Phillips

The Father has loved us so much! He loved us so much that we are called children of God. And we really are his children. But the people in the world do not understand that we are God's children, because they have not known him ~ 1 John 3:1 (International Children's Bible-ICB)

About the book:

Honey and Mahogany is an inspiring story for children that emphasizes the joy of being biracial. The different shades of biracial children are highlighted in this book and showing how children need to be proud of the shade of their skin and being the children of parents who look different. When the love of family and pride of who you are shines through, children can understand not to mind when prejudice comes their way.

First there was dad,

the Creole King.

Then he met mom,
the Snow Fairy Queen.

The two fell in love, creating a happy and special family.

As the children grew up, they started noticing others would look and stare at their family while they walk down the street or play at the park.

They ask Mommy and Daddy, "why do people look at us so much?"

"Well children," as Daddy says in his strong and caring voice. "They just cannot get enough of your unique and beautiful skin colors." "But why Daddy?" Ella asks. "Because our family is special, my little Rich Mahogany Princess and my little Honey Bronze Prince."

"Cookies are ready, gather around" Mommy announced. "My sweet babies, I want the two of you to feel proud when others stare at you, because what they see is one happy and loving family."

Just like older brothers do, they try to make their little sisters smile. "Ella, you look more like Daddy, and I look more like Mommy," Devon says. "Look at this chocolate cookie. Without milk it is just a regular cookie, nothing special at all. Now, when you dunk the cookie and mix it with milk, it becomes the most special and best dessert there is!"

"That's right Devon," Mommy and Daddy say. "You two are special, unique, and have a very special place in this world. Special like the dessert with the cookie and the milk mixed together," Mommy says in her sweet voice.

Daddy explains to Devon, "you have the sweetness from your mother like honey and the strength of bronze from me. That makes you Honey Bronze."

"Now Princess, as my daughter, you have the strength from me like a Mahogany tree, and you are rare and polished like your Mommy. That makes you Rich Mahogany."

"Both of you are special and have the love and protection from both Daddy and me," Mommy says with a smile.

Both Devon and Ella look at their parents and ask, "after we finish our cookies and milk, can we go for a walk to the park to show everyone how proud we are to be us? We want to show everyone how proud we are to have you as our Mommy and Daddy. PLEEEASSSSEE!?!"

"That is a wonderful idea," both parents proclaim.

The children grab their jackets and run out the front door, waiting on their parents to hurry up.

Side by side holding hands, the family strolls down the sidewalk.

An elderly couple stops in front of the family and before they had time to stare or say hello to the children, the children scream loud and proud…

"I am Honey Bronze, and this is my sister, Rich Mahogany," Devon says. "We are the best features mixed together from both our Daddy and our Mommy," both children say.

The elderly couple looks at the parents and say, "it is so wonderful to see that your children are so proud of their skin tones. You make a beautiful family!"

The parents start walking towards their kids, who have ran onto the playground swings. Mommy and Daddy look at their Honey Bronze Prince and Rich Mahogany Princess, and replies with the biggest smiles on their faces, "all we see is a loving family, which we are very proud of indeed."

About the Author:

Heather R. Phillips loves writing children's books to inspire! She writes stories hoping to inspire children who are born from multiple cultures to embrace where they come from and be proud of who they are and how they look to the world. With a warm and happy story, Heather hopes that children want to read her books again and again while inspiring them to walk around proudly about where they come from. In her professional life, she pursues a dedicated career fighting for social/racial equity and justice. She hopes to captivate and inspire a young audience through her children's books on the topics she has dedicated her life to.

Illustration Credits:

Theresa Thompson-Cisco

CPSIA information can be obtained
at www.ICGtesting.com
Printed in the USA
LVHW070327031121
702215LV00009B/195